ZEKE

———————

EYE CANDY INK BOOK 4

SHAW HART

BLURB

Zeke Miller is the owner of Eye Candy Ink and the father figure to everyone at the shop. An only child who had to grow up far too young, he's always felt protective of those he loves.

He's spent years building Eye Candy Ink into what it is today. While others dated and settled down, he worked, honing his skills until he's one of the best and most sought after tattoo artists in the world. At thirty-six, he thinks his time to meet someone has passed and he's resigned to being happy with the family that he's found at his shop.

Then Trixie Jones comes into Eye Candy Ink. She has all of his protective instincts kicking in. But none of them are fatherly.

1

Z eke

"ZEKE!" Sam calls from up front and I pause my conversation with Max. I know that Mischa and Nico are both with clients and I'm guessing Sam's got one and needs me to fill in for her at the front desk.

"Hey, man, I'll have to call you back. Your girlfriend needs me."

"Hilarious," he says back and I chuckle before I tell him I'll talk to him later and hang up.

I push some of my dirty blond locks out of my face, which reminds me that I could probably use a haircut soon as I head down the hallway. I pass by Mischa's room and peek inside to see him bent over some girl's leg. He's blaring some rock song that I don't recognize and I smile when I look over to his desk and see a picture of him and Indie in a frame. I'm sure that was Indie's doing since Mischa is more of a pushpin in the wall kind of guy. He looks up and nods at me as I walk up to the front counter.

Nico's door is closed and I remember that he had some big shot celebrity client this morning. He hates tattooing celebrities but he's the best out there, after me of course, so it's no surprise that they want him.

Sam is sitting behind the counter, her bright pink hair shining in the light as she types something into the computer and I look across the desk at, who I'm assuming, is her client.

My breath catches in my lungs as I take in the girl standing there. I say girl because that's exactly what she is. She's tiny, probably only a few inches past five feet, with wavy platinum blonde hair that hangs halfway down her back. She looks like an angel standing there in her white Keds and floral sundress.

She's the most beautiful, well, anything that I've seen in my life. I'm an artist and I know beauty. This girl is meant to be painted, to be worshipped. Her mouth is curled up into a friendly smile, her lips a perfect pillowy bow. She blinks up at me, her pale lashes framing a pair of bright sea green eyes. I can see interest and intelligence in her eyes and I want to step closer to her, to know what she smells like, what she tastes like.

She shifts, biting her lip and my cock grows two sizes in my jeans. I clear my throat, realizing that I've just been staring at her for the past few minutes.

"Can I help you?" I ask, wanting to hear her speak, wanting to have her eyes on me.

I move closer to the desk so that I can hide the bulge in my jeans as she turns and smiles softly at me but before she can open her mouth, Sam pipes up.

"She's working on an assignment for school and was wondering if you could help."

"School?" I ask, panic taking over me. *Please god, let this girl be eighteen.*

"Yeah, I'm a sophomore over at Carnegie Mellon University," she says, her lyrical voice coming out soft.

"Oh thank god," I mumble and Sam gives me a weird look. "What's the assignment?" I ask, trying to get my cock to go down. My jeans are strangling it and I'm worried that I'm going to have an imprint of my zipper along it for the rest of my life.

"I'm taking an art class and we're supposed to go out and find examples of art that people wouldn't normally see as art. I thought of tattoos and was wondering if I could learn more about the process and see some of the designs."

I'm nodding my head before she even finishes. Any excuse to spend more time with this girl, I'm going to take.

"Sure, let me show you around the shop. I'm Zeke, by the way," I say, adjusting my jeans as I walk around to open the gate for her.

"Trixie," she says with a shy smile as she meets me outside the gate.

I see Sam pull out her phone and I have a feeling I know who she's texting. Sure enough, approximately five seconds later, Nico and Mischa's doors both pop open and they look out with shocked faces as I usher Trixie into the back. Nico recovers first and just nods his head before he shuts his door again. Mischa...not so much.

I groan under my breath as we walk closer to him and he starts to grin in that crazy way of his. I shoot him a warning look and he pouts, rolling his eyes before he darts back into his room. I shoot a glare over my shoulder at Sam and she smirks back at me. This is probably payback for giving Max her number all those weeks ago.

I lead Trixie back to my office and tell her she can leave her bag in here if she doesn't want to carry it around the whole time. She sets it in one of the chairs, smiling at me and I swear my heart tries to beat out of my chest.

I'll admit, I had been feeling jealous these last few months. Seeing Atlas and then Mischa, MISCHA, settle down had made me wonder if maybe I was missing something. I had been worried that Mischa would die alone but now I'm in danger of meeting that fate. When Sam and Max first got together, I had decided that maybe I should try dating too. I just had no idea where to start or how to go about it. I mean I'm thirty-six. The last time I took a girl out was before I opened Eye Candy Ink and that was over a decade ago.

I never really noticed how lonely I was. I had the shop to run and I was too busy trying to grow my business to see that the rest of my life had kind of fallen by the wayside. I had a family, people that I loved and cared about and who loved and cared about me too. It's not the same though and watching everyone else pair up has made me see that.

I had seriously been considering online dating but every time I would go to type in the website name, something would stop me. Maybe it's an age thing but finding someone online just seems so strange to me. I wasn't even sure how to fill out one of the forms. How do you describe yourself in just a few short sentences? How do you know what you're looking for? To me, that connection happens in real life, not from seeing a picture of someone on some website.

Although, I think if I had seen a picture of Trixie online, I still would have had this reaction.

"I'm ready," she says as she pulls out a little notebook and a pen.

"Me too," I mumble as I lead her back out into the hallway.

2

T rixie

I DON'T KNOW what I was expecting the owner of a tattoo shop to look like but this Viking lookalike wasn't it. His chin length dirty blond hair hangs in waves around his tanned face. He's older than me, I would guess in his mid-thirties, although when I first saw him, I thought he was only a few years older than me. When I got closer, I could see the wrinkles around his eyes and mouth better and the few gray hairs mixed in with the blond.

I've never been that interested in the opposite sex, probably because I grew up with a mother who liked to drill how terrible men were into me since I was a young girl. My dad left before I was born, leaving my mother bitter and with a little girl to raise by herself.

Growing up with her had been tough at times. She was a strict woman, always trying to dictate my life and what I should and shouldn't do. I guess I shouldn't say trying to. She still controls me, even when there's hundreds of miles between us.

When it had come time for me to apply to colleges, she had picked out a few private universities close to home and Carnegie Mellon, her Alma Mater. I had snuck in the Art Institute of Chicago. I got into all of them and I was dying to go to art school but my mother told me that wouldn't be practical. Instead, I found myself being packed up and moved to Pittsburgh.

Instead of art, I'm studying business, a subject that I couldn't care less about and one that I'm not even particularly good at. My mother tells me that it will be a good degree, one that will be versatile and therefore provide for more job opportunities.

I'd rather be an artist. I've always loved to draw and paint but my mother says it's just a hobby. A useless hobby, are her exact words. She picked all of my classes my freshman year but I lied to her this year and told her that my guidance counselors had recommended some classes for me. That wasn't a complete lie and I did sign up for some of the business classes that they suggested but I was also able to pick some of my own classes this term. I snuck an art class in and I'm just waiting for my mother to find out and freak out at me. It will be worth it though. My soul was dying sitting through all of those dreary math courses.

Zeke leads me to the back of the building and into what I'm guessing is his office.

"You can set your bag in here," he offers and I gladly take him up on it.

My bag weighs about fifty pounds with all of my textbooks in it and it was starting to hurt my shoulder. I dig inside pulling out a notebook and pen before I turn back to him. He smiles at me as we make our way back out into the hallway. There's art and tattoo designs on the walls and we stop in front of the first one. I study the piece, taking in the thick brushstrokes and the vivid use of color. It's an abstract, a style that I don't normally love but there's something beautiful about this piece.

"Do you like it?" He asks, his voice quiet in the hallway.

It's a little hard to hear him over the noise of music playing and the tattoo machines and I move closer to him. He smells like ink and paper and it's comforting.

"I do. Who is the artist? Someone local?"

"It's one of Nico's. The guy in the front room," he says, nodding his head toward a room up by the front counter.

I remember the guy who had stuck his head out when I first got here and I smile.

"He's very talented. Are all of these his? Or are some of them yours?" I ask, pointing around to some of the other art displayed on the walls.

"Some of them are Nico's. Some are local artists who we agreed to display. I don't have any of mine hanging here."

"It's cool that you do that. For the locals, I mean."

He just shrugs at that, looking away at the compliment.

"When did you get into tattoos?"

"Before I was legally able to," he says with a wry grin.

"Really?" I ask, growing intrigued.

"Yeah, I grew up in Vegas and there wasn't much else for a scrawny little punk kid to do."

"Have you always known that you wanted to be a tattoo artist?"

"Pretty much," he says with a little shrug. "I always liked drawing but I didn't come from much. I never would have made it selling art. Besides, I needed money then and it was easy to make a quick hundred bucks or so back then for tattooing people at parties."

"It was probably good practice."

He smiles at that and I have to hold back my sigh. He's so good looking but it becomes ridiculous when he smiles. No one should be allowed to be that hot.

"So what brought you to Pittsburgh?" I ask and I wonder if he realizes that I've asked more questions about him than about tattooing or art.

"I left Vegas as soon as I turned eighteen and kind of bounced around from shop to shop for a while. I was out in California for a few years, apprenticing and working for some of the best artists there are but after a while, they couldn't teach me anything else and I got tired of working for other people. I had a friend from Vegas who moved up here for college and he invited me to crash on his couch."

"And then you opened Eye Candy Ink?" I ask as he leans back against the wall.

"Kinda. I was on his couch for a few weeks, trying to figure some things out, but Max is a go getter. He owns a few restaurants and he offered to invest in my tattoo shop. The next thing I knew he was showing me realtor listings. He helped me find this building and then I hired Nico," he says nodding toward a door up front. "Mischa, Sam, and Atlas, came after, once we were already more settled."

"Why did you name it Eye Candy Ink?" I ask and Zeke chuckles, the sound rasping over my skin like a caress. I've always been curious about that. I've heard the rumors about how everyone has to be hot to work here but Zeke doesn't seem like that kind of guy. He cares about the work, about the shop's reputation too much to hire a less than talented artist to work for him.

"I lost a bet and Max got to name it. He was pretty drunk

when he came up with it but a bet's a bet. The bright pink sign was up the next week."

I smile at that. It's nice to see that Zeke is a man of his word and part of me wants to introduce him to my mom, just so I can show her that she doesn't have to hate all men. Some of them are still good guys.

Zeke shows me some of the other art hanging on the wall and we spend over an hour in that hallway. It's been the most fun I've had since I came to Pittsburgh. Maybe even ever.

He offers to buy me dinner but it's getting late and I need to get back to my dorm room. I still have a few papers and homework assignments that I need to finish tonight and as much as I would like to stay here and talk to Zeke, listening to him tell me more about the art in this place or discussing some of our favorite artists or pieces, I know that I need to go.

"You know, we didn't actually get around to talking about tattoos tonight," Zeke says as he carries my backpack up to the front door for me. He frowned when he picked it up and I could tell that he wanted to say something about how heavy it was but he kept it to himself.

"Maybe I could come back soon so we can go over that?" I ask, blushing. I've never been that bold before but Zeke seems to like it.

"Anytime, Trix," he says as he holds the front door open for me.

I think I smile the whole way back to campus.

3

Zeke

TODAY IS my day off but I've been coming in every day for the last few days in the hopes that Trixie comes back into the shop. I've been kicking myself for not getting her phone number or making definite plans for a day for her to come back. I keep having nightmares that she went to a different shop and someone else steals her from me.

I lean back in my chair. I haven't been able to get much work done the last few days and I know that I need to push thoughts of Trixie from my head so that I can get payroll done. It's proving to be harder than I thought.

I run my fingers through my hair, tugging slightly on the ends as I turn back to my computer. I'm just about to open the accounting program when my door bangs open and Mischa bounces in. I try to hide my grin because I already know that he's here to give me shit.

"As Eye Candy Ink's resident ladies' man, I'm here to give you some pointers," he announces as he collapses into the chair across the desk from me.

"You almost lost Indie," Nico reminds him as he files into the room after him.

"But I didn't and now look at us," Mischa says, spreading his arms wide and smacking Nico in the arm as he crams his body into the chair next to Mischa.

"What are we talking about?" Atlas asks as he wanders into the room as well.

He leans against Mischa's chair, smiling at his phone as he types something out.

"As I was saying," Mischa says, shooting an annoyed look at Nico and Atlas. "As Eye Candy Ink's resident ladies' man,-"

"Who named you ladies' man?" Atlas asks, shoving his phone into his pocket.

"Uh, I helped you get Darcy, didn't I?"

"You mean when you sent me all of those dating articles?" Atlas asks with a chuckle.

"No, but that was good. Don't worry, Dad. I still have them. I'll email them to you tonight."

"Thanks," I say drily but part of me wonders if I *should* take a look at them. Then the rational side of my brain kicks in and reminds me that I'm too old for her and I need to get her off my mind.

"No problem," Mischa says at the same time Atlas tells me that I don't need them.

"They didn't help me at all. Mischa is the worst with girls. He almost lost Indie," Atlas says and I see Nico hide his smile behind his hand.

"BUT I DIDN'T AND NOW WE'RE IN LOVE!" Mischa shouts and Atlas grins at him.

"I think he meant he helped you with Darcy because he was the one who went and talked to her after she broke up with you," I say and I watch Atlas's smile fade.

"You did?" He asks quietly, and Mischa blushes, shifting nervously in his chair.

"Yeah, but only because I couldn't stand to live with you when you were moping around."

"I don't think that's it. I think you're the most romantic of all of us," I tease and Mischa shoots me a glare.

"Absolutely not. I hate romance," he insists.

"Indie is one lucky girl," Nico deadpans and Atlas laughs.

"Anyway... I just wanted to say that as Eye Candy Ink's resident ladies' man—"

"You're not a ladies man," Atlas, Nico, and I all say in unison.

"I just wanted you to know that I'm here if you have any questions," Mischa finishes.

"Thanks, son."

I can tell that they want to ask me about Trixie but before they can, Sam yells down the hallway.

"Hey! Are any of you working?"

Mischa and Nico stand and I nod at Atlas and Mischa as they filter out of my office and back to their rooms. Atlas throws his arm around Mischa's neck, tugging him into a side hug as they walk back to their rooms. I see him say something to him as they walk away and I'm assuming he's thanking him for going to see Darcy.

Nico stays behind, looking down the hallway before he looks back to me.

"Are you dating now?" He asks quietly.

"I think I'm going to try to." My mind flits back to the dating websites and I feel like a part of me dies just picturing filling out one of those forms. I need to find someone my own age though, no matter if it feels like my heart only wants one girl.

Nico nods, shoving his hands into his jeans as he frowns at his shoes.

"What about you, Nico? Ever thought about settling down?"

"I am settled," he says, looking up and meeting my eyes.

That's true. Out of all of us, Nico is probably the most settled, the most consistent.

"I meant, are you thinking about finding your own girl?"

He gives me a noncommittal shrug and my eyebrow rises. Nico always has an answer. He's very realistic, sees the world in very clear, black and white terms.

"You're not really going to take dating advice from Mischa, are you?" He asks me and I grin.

"Absolutely not."

He grins back at me, knocking on the doorframe twice before he heads back to his room. I turn back to my computer but I don't get very far before Sam is calling my name.

"Zeke! Visitor!"

My heart leaps in my chest and I groan. I need to get myself under control. *You're old enough to be her father,* I remind myself as I run my hands through my hair and down my shirt, trying to keep cool as I head out to see who is here.

Please let it be Trixie.

4

T rixie

I HAD WAITED a few days before I went back to see Zeke at Eye Candy Ink. My project isn't due for another two weeks and I didn't want to seem desperate. That's a thing, right? I've never been allowed to date or have a boyfriend before and I don't really know how to behave or act around him.

After one day, I was starting to get antsy. I mean he never said when I should come back and he didn't ask for my number, so maybe I just imagined this connection between us. Maybe he was just being kind to me when he showed me around. He seems like a good guy so he could have just been being nice to a poor college student.

After two days, I had bounced back to feeling like there was definitely something between us. I had never had problems concentrating before but suddenly, Zeke was all that I could think about. He might be close to twice my age, but my heart doesn't care. There's something between us. I know it.

After three days, I couldn't take it any longer. I looked it up and the only rule I could find was a forty-eight hour wait time rule. As soon as I saw that, I was pulling on my shoes and grabbing my backpack.

It's only a couple of blocks walk to Eye Candy Ink and with only a few notebooks and pens, my backpack is a lot lighter today. My palms start to sweat as I get closer to the tattoo shop and I take a deep breath, giving myself a mental pep talk. I'm almost to the door when I run into someone.

I look up, an apology on my lips, but the other person beats me to it. A beautiful curvy blonde and her friend, a black haired, willowy girl are standing there.

"I'm sorry," the curvy blonde says, her voice quiet and melodic.

"I think it was my fault actually. I wasn't watching where I was going. Sorry," I say and both girls smile at me.

"Are you headed into Eye Candy? Are you getting a tattoo?" The black-haired girl asks, her voice excited. Her enthusiasm is infectious and I feel a smile tugging at my lips.

"Yeah, I'm here to see Zeke about my art project," I tell them.

"Oh! You're Trixie!" The black-haired girl says, her purple eyes seeming to glow in her pale face.

"Yeah, how did you-" I start to ask but before I can finish my sentence, the girl has already grabbed my arm and dragged me into the shop.

Her friend follows after us and I can hear her chuckling. The girl holding onto my arm drags me over to the red velvet couch in the corner of the lobby and pulls me down to sit next to her. Sam, the girl behind the counter, grins when she sees us and I see her glance over her shoulder toward the back rooms.

"I'm Indie and this is Darcy," Indie says, pointing to her friend who is sitting in the chair next to me.

"Hi," I say, unsure about who they are.

"Zeke hasn't told you about us?" Indie asks, her voice raising with outrage.

I hear a door open down the hall and two sets of footsteps come our way.

Two guys appear at the metal gate, one grinning like a lunatic and the other with a soft smile on his face. Indie and Darcy both stand and make their way over to them, Indie skipping and throwing herself at the one with the wild smile and while Darcy just walks up and wraps her arms around the other guy.

"Zeke! Visitor!" Sam yells and my stomach tightens as I wait to get another peek at Zeke.

I'm dying to know if that attraction, that connection I felt the first time I saw him is still there.

"Did you know that Zeke didn't even tell Trixie about us?" Indie asks the guy she's wrapped around.

"I don't think they've done much talking like that," the guy says and Indie's eyes open wide.

She wiggles away and comes back over to me, raising her hand for a high-five.

"Not like that!" The guy says through his laughter.

"They've only met once. Right?" The other guy says, turning to look at me.

"Sorry, I think I missed something here," I say, rising to my feet and shifting nervously.

"Ignore them," Zeke says as he opens the gate and my core tightens at the powerful sound of his voice.

My thighs clench together and I give him a little smile as

he comes over to my side. I'm dwarfed by his size but it makes me feel protected.

"Trixie, this lunatic is Mischa," he says, pointing to the guy who has wrapped his arms around Indie again. He waves at me and I wave back.

"And this is Atlas," he says and I wave at the other guy who has his arm wrapped around Darcy's shoulders.

"Nice to meet you both," I say and they both smile at me.

"Don't you both have clients to prepare for?" Zeke asks and they mumble before they turn and all head back to their rooms. Indie and Darcy both wave at me over their shoulders and Indie holds her hand up in a call me motion. I can't help but grin at that.

"Sorry about them. They can be a little... overenthusiastic," Zeke says.

"No, I liked them," I tell him and he smiles down at me, reaching out to push a stray lock of hair away from my face.

The act is intimate and catches me off guard, but I recover quickly and have to force myself not to lean into his touch.

"Ready for another tour?" He asks me after a minute, clearing his throat as he takes a step away from me. I want to follow after him, to close the distance he just put between us, but I force myself to remain still.

"Ready," I say, digging a notebook and pen from my backpack.

He reaches out and takes my backpack, smiling slightly when he feels it isn't as heavy as it was the last time. I follow after him as he leads me back to his office where he puts my backpack down in a chair.

"This way. I'll show you my room," he says, placing his hand on the small of my back and leading me up to a room close to the front.

"Do you have any tattoos?" He asks as he closes the door behind us, blocking out some of the other noise.

"No," I say with a slight laugh. "My mother would kill me."

He watches me curiously for a second before he smiles. "Would you like one?"

His question catches me off guard. I've never really thought about it. I just always knew that my mother would never let me.

"I don't know," I say slowly.

Zeke watches me for a moment, his bright blue eyes assessing me before he smiles, flashing his straight white teeth at me.

"Let me walk you through the process," he says and he turns toward a desk and begins to pull out some supplies and equipment.

We spend the next two hours in that room. Zeke walks me through how to tattoo someone, from learning what the client wants and drawing up a sketch of the tattoo to what ointments to put on once the tattoo is done. He tells me about the different styles of tattoos, where they each originated from and shows me examples of each. I take pictures and write down notes on each, knowing that I'm going to ace this project and this class.

Zeke is an incredible artist. I swear that my breath gets taken away when he shows me some of the designs that he's made. My fingers itch for my own supplies. I wonder if I could recreate some of his designs for my project. Some of his pieces spark my creativity and a hundred different ideas pop into my head.

A knock sounds at the door and I startle in my chair. Mischa opens it and pokes his head in.

"Sorry to interrupt, but it's closing time. We're all headed out."

I look down at my phone and see it's after 9 pm. I close my notebook and stand. Zeke frowns at me but stands too.

"Nice to meet you, Trixie," Mischa says before he turns to leave and I smile at him.

"You too," I say, waving as he leaves.

"Let's get your backpack and I'll drive you back to campus," Zeke says, placing his hand on the small of my back and leading me back to his office.

"You don't have to do that. It's not that far. I can walk," I try to protest.

"Trix, I'm not letting you walk anywhere at night by yourself."

I smile at my shoes, reaching for my backpack. I shove my notebook and pen inside, zipping it up. I go to pull it onto my shoulders when Zeke reaches out and grabs the strap. He smiles at me as he grabs my hand in his large one and leads me out of the shop and over to his car. It's a newer model, black, Ford Explorer and as we get closer, I wonder how I'm going to be able to climb up inside.

Before I can worry too much, Zeke has grabbed my hips and he lifts me, helping me inside. I tense as he picks me off the ground and my whole body tingles at his touch. I love how big he is and how he can just pick me up and move me where he wants me. I bite my bottom lip, trying to get the butterflies in my stomach under control.

5

Z eke

TRIXIE WAS quiet on the way back to her dorm, staring out the window and only speaking to give me directions. She directs me into a parking lot across the street from her dorm building and I circle the lot trying to find an open spot. The only one available is in the back row and I pull in shutting off the car as Trixie gathers her backpack.

"Thanks for the ride," she says in her sweet voice.

"I'll walk you to your room," I tell her, climbing out of my car.

"You don't have to," she tries to protest but it's dark and there's only a few streetlights on the way to her building.

"I want to," I tell her and it's the truth.

I want to take care of this girl. To make sure that she's safe and cared for. Maybe it's my paternal instincts, although most of the thoughts that I'm having about this girl are decidedly not fatherly.

I help her out of the SUV and take her bag from her, intertwining my fingers with hers as we walk over to her dorm. She lives on the first floor and I frown at that.

"Do you like your roommate?" I ask, as we walk down the hallway toward her room.

"I actually have three roommates. I haven't spent that much time with them. They have later classes and mine are all in the morning and they seem to go out a lot at night."

Sounds like party girls and I frown harder at the thought of them around my sweet girl. We arrive outside her room and I hold her backpack out to her as she rummages inside of one of the compartments for her keys. She gives me a smile when she finds them and I can't help but return it.

I wait for her to open the door, intending to carry her bag inside for her and make sure that her room is safe but as soon as she swings the door open, I'm jumping in front of her and slamming it shut.

Trixie looks shocked, her face turning a pretty cherry red and I look from her and back to the door.

"Do you usually come home to two naked guys walking around your dorm room?" I ask, trying to keep the anger I feel out of my voice.

"Uh, no. This would be a first," she says, looking embarrassed and uneasy.

"Come on. You can sleep at my place," I tell her as I take her hand in mine and lead her back out to my SUV.

I notice that she doesn't try to argue with me and I'm not sure if it's because she likes the idea of staying with me or if she just really didn't want to stay there with those two strange boys.

I actually live close to the campus in a converted warehouse. I bought it a couple of years ago when I got sick of living in my cramped apartment. I wanted more room but I didn't want to live out of the city limits. This way, I have space and I'm still close to Eye Candy Ink.

I pull up outside, hitting the button for the door to open and I drive inside, parking close to the stairs. I shut the SUV off and turn to see Trixie looking around the space. There's not much to see on this floor. It's all concrete and steel although I have spray painted some designs on the walls. I took up graffiti last year, looking to expand my skills as an artist but I only ever did it around here. Now the first floor of my place is covered in it.

Trixie hops out of the car before I can get around to help her and I see her go over to one of the walls. Her eyes are huge, almost as big as her smile as she walks around the space, taking in the bright designs on the walls.

I let her look, trailing after her as she makes a loop around the ground floor. When we get back to the stairs, she turns to face me.

"Are these all yours?"

"Yeah, I've been working on them in my spare time," I tell her as I place my hand in the small of her back and lead her upstairs. I open the door and lead her inside.

I redid this whole space after I bought it, adding copper fixtures and comfy leather couches. The top floor is just as open as the first floor and you can see everything, the kitchen, living room, and my bed over in the back corner. My bathroom and closet are back there too and that's the only doors in the place.

"Nice place," she says, walking further into the space.

"Thanks. Are you hungry?" I ask as I head over to the kitchen.

"I could eat," she says, giving me a soft smile.

I open the fridge, pulling out some stuff to make sandwiches. It's getting late and I know Trixie must be tired after a day of classes and then hanging out at the shop. I want her to get to bed soon so she can get a full night's rest and be prepared for her classes tomorrow.

Thoughts of us spooned in my bed, both of us flushed with passion, float through my mind and I clear my throat, turning to grab some bread from the cabinet. I shouldn't be having thoughts like that about Trixie. She just came to me for help with a class. I might want more from her but that doesn't mean that she feels the same way as me. Besides, I'm almost old enough to be her dad. That's probably how she sees me. As a father figure or mentor.

Why does that thought break my heart a little bit?

T rixie

ZEKE SLIDES a plate in front of me and my mouth waters as I take in the sandwich and chips piled high on the plate. My mother would never let me eat junk food like this and I smile, loving the fact that Zeke wants me to. He takes the seat next to me, his own plate filled with food and he smiles at me before he picks up his own sandwich and bites in. I follow his lead, moaning as the first bite of sandwich hits my tongue. I swear I hear Zeke groan but I'm too hungry to stop eating and check.

I clear my plate quickly and smile at Zeke as he slides his plate closer to me. We polish off the last of his chips and then Zeke carries the dishes over to the sink.

"I'll get you a change of clothes," he says as he walks over to the bedroom area in the back.

He rummages inside the closet for a second, pulling out

a t-shirt with Eye Candy Ink written on the front and a pair
of sweatpants. He shows me where the bathroom is and I
close the door, stripping off my clothes. With my belly full,
my eyes are growing heavy and I have a feeling that I'm
going to fall asleep soon.

I tug his shirt over my head, bringing the fabric to my
nose and breathing deeply. It smells like him and I smile. I
try to pull his sweatpants on but they're way too big,
covering my feet and falling off my waist. I try to roll them
up a few times but that still doesn't help. In the end, I decide
that his shirt will be enough. It comes down to mid-thigh
and I know it's late so we're probably going to be going to
bed anyway.

I fold my clothes up and leave them on the bathroom
vanity before I pad back out into the bedroom. Zeke is over
by the couch, smoothing out a blanket and I notice that
there's already some pillows over there too.

"I'll take the couch," he says as I walk closer and I swear
I see him gulp.

"Don't be silly. You're way too big to fit on there."

"I'll be fine," he tells me.

I frown as he smooths the blanket out over the back, I
sneak up next to him. As soon as he steps back, I jump onto
the cushions, curling up on my side and burying my head in
the pillow.

I grin up at him and I can see a pained look on Zeke's
face.

"Tuck me in?" I ask and I swear I see his eyes heat at my
words.

He nods slightly, reaching over me and pulling the
blanket down to cover me. He tucks it around my shoulders,
before he moves down my body, pausing slightly when he

gets to my bare legs. He tucks the blankets under my feet, making sure that I'm all wrapped up before he steps back.

"Are you warm enough, Trix?" He asks me as he takes another step back.

My toes curl at the nickname and I feel a tingling starting in my pussy. I nod up at him, peeking out at him from behind the blanket. He's got it wrapped around me so tightly that I can barely move and I love how worried he is about me. I love that he keeps asking if I'm okay or if I want something.

I can't remember the last time that someone asked me what *I* thought. My mother always just tells me what to think or how to feel about stuff. Even my professors are doing the same thing, although they're trying to teach me.

Zeke is different. He makes me feel important and smart while also making me feel protected and cared for. I've never had someone who made me feel like that before and I don't want to lose it.

I snuggle deeper into the blankets, my eyelashes fluttering closed as I feel sleep start to claim me. I can hear Zeke moving around over by the bed but I'm too tired to really pay attention to what he's doing.

I'm just about to drift under when I hear Zeke.

"Goodnight, Trix," he says, his deep voice rasping over my skin and making me smile.

"Night, Zeke," I mumble before I let sleep claim me.

Z eke

I WAKE the next morning to the smell of sugar and my whole body stiffens, especially a specific part of my body. I want to roll over, but I'm afraid Trixie will be getting more of an eyeful than she anticipated.

I didn't sleep well last night. I didn't expect that I would, not after I saw her in nothing but my t-shirt. I could smell her in my space and when I walked into the bathroom and saw her bra on top of her clothes, I swear I just about came in my pants. Then she cuddled up on my couch and fell asleep. The sight of her bare legs had me biting back a groan.

I had a hard on for hours after that. My cock had been begging for release but I didn't want to risk it. Not with her sleeping just a few feet away. I stared at my ceiling for hours, listening to her even breathing until finally, I fell asleep.

Now, I'm hard as steel again and I just woke up. I grit my teeth, rolling over in bed and sitting up. I blink my eyes, adjusting to the light and I smile when I see Trixie in the kitchen. She's got a spatula in one hand and a bowl in the other and I realize that she's making pancakes.

She turns and sees me sitting up and she blushes slightly as she waves the spatula at me.

"Morning," she says and I throw my legs over the side of the bed.

"Morning."

"I made breakfast," she says and I walk closer, noting the pile of pancakes on the counter.

"It smells delicious," I say, walking up behind her and grabbing some plates out of the cabinet and a couple of glasses.

We move in sync, her turning off the stove and moving the pan as I pour us each a glass of orange juice and set two places on the counter. I find the syrup and set that out too as she carries everything over to the table.

The pancakes are delicious and we make small talk about her classes and what her plans are for today. She tells me she needs to work on her art project and tells me more about it as we do up the dishes. It's obvious that the art class is her favorite class and I want to ask her why she's taking business classes at all but before I can, Trixie is racing into the bathroom and coming back out in her clothes.

I miss seeing her in my shirt but I don't say anything, just smile as I grab my keys and help her down the stairs and out into the car.

"Did you want me to drop you off at your dorm room or at your class?" I ask as we head the few blocks to campus.

"My dorm room please. I need to grab my books and stuff and change my clothes."

I nod, pulling into the same parking lot as last night. I help Trixie out of the car and hold her hand as we walk across campus to her building. I know I don't need to walk her in today, but part of me wants to go check and make sure that those boys from last night are gone.

Trixie reaches for the doorknob and I bite back a growl of annoyance when I see that the door was unlocked. I follow Trixie inside, looking around but it looks like everyone is gone or in their bedrooms.

"Thanks for walking me to my door. And for letting me stay at your place last night. And for the food," she says, smiling shyly.

"It was my pleasure, Trix. You're welcome anytime."

"Thanks," she says, looking down at her shoes and I know that I should leave.

"Good luck with your assignment. Let me know if you need any more help with it," I tell her, taking a step back toward the door.

"Thanks. I'll text you," she says and then she blushes. "I mean, I'll come see you. Sorry."

"Here, give me your phone."

She hands it over and I bring up a new contact, typing in my name and number and sending myself a text before I hand it back to her.

"There, now you can call or text me too."

"Thanks, Zeke," she says and I nod, taking another step back.

"I'll see you around, Trixie," I say as I head out the door.

"See you, Zeke."

She waves at me as I close the door after me and I let out a sigh as I stand out in the hallway. As soon as the door closes, I want to bang my head against it. I might be out of practice but even I know that that didn't go well. I smile at some girls who are headed my way, cringing when they giggle behind me.

"Fuck. Maybe I should look at those dating articles Mischa sent me," I mumble under my breath as I head outside and back to my car.

8

Trixie

I KNOW it's not fair, but I feel like this is Zeke's fault.

I wince when someone digs their elbow into my side, trying to keep my roommates in my sight in the crowded bar. They had invited me out with them tonight and I didn't know what to say. Part of me knew that it wasn't a good idea but I was sick of sitting around my dorm room, daydreaming about Zeke and the dirty things I'd like him to do to me.

I had hoped that maybe this was a turning point and they were finally trying to be friends with me but it's becoming clear that that's not the case. They've barely looked in my direction since we got here. Instead, I've been following after them like a lost puppy dog. It's too loud in here to hear them and it's so crowded that I keep losing sight of them.

We're headed to the bar now. I think. We had to walk around the dancefloor and I saw one of my roommates, Heather, break off and head toward the bathroom. When I looked forward again, I had lost sight of the other two girls. I stand on my tiptoes, trying to peer over the crowd when someone knocks into me from behind. I stumble forward, almost running into a bar stool as I struggle to keep my balance.

When I right myself and look around, I've completely lost sight of my roommates. Part of me wants to scream and the other just wants to cry. I knew that I shouldn't have come out with them. I debate going to find them and tell them that I want to leave but I know that they won't really care and I don't want to spend another hour looking around the place for them.

I trip and stumble my way to the front door, squeezing between a few guys and bursting outside onto the sidewalk. It's starting to drizzle and I tip my head back, letting the drops mist over my face and cool me off.

"Trixie?" I hear and I drop my head down, my eyes meeting Zeke's.

I feel dizzy at the sight of him. He's at the red light and I lift my hand in a wave. He doesn't look happy to see me. He glares at me, his eyes flicking between me and the dive bar behind me that I obviously just came out of. I reach up, my nervous fingers trying to smooth my hair down.

"Get in," Zeke orders and my body tightens at the command. I'm walking before I even realize I gave my body the order.

Zeke leans across the console, opening the passenger door for me. I close the door right as the light turns green but Zeke waits for me to buckle up before he takes off.

"What are you doing in this area?" I ask when I notice that he's driving away from his place and campus.

"What am *I* doing in this area? What are *YOU* doing in this area? What are you doing in a place like that?" He asks, his voice coming out tight with anger.

"My roommates invited me out with them tonight but it wasn't as much fun as I thought it was going to be," I admit, my voice getting lost in the rain on the roof of the car. It's starting to come down harder now and Zeke swears as he hits the windshield wipers, slowing down in the traffic.

"Were you drinking?"

"I just had a sip of beer. I don't know how anyone can drink that stuff. It tasted terrible," I say, gagging just thinking about the bitter taste.

"You aren't old enough to drink and you shouldn't be out in a place like that. What if someone had put something in your drink? What if the cops had come and you had gotten arrested? How could you do that?" He asks, his anger returning.

"I just had a sip. I'm fine and I won't be going back there. Trust me," I tell him, my own anger starting to rise as he continues to berate me.

"You shouldn't have been in there in the first place," he mumbles under his breath and I see red.

"Why are you over here, Zeke? Were you out at some bar too?" I ask, turning in my seat to face him.

"God, no. Those places are dives," he says with a look of disgust.

"Then why are you over here? Eye Candy Ink and your place are about eight blocks that way," I say pointing out the rearview window.

"Darcy called Atlas. She thought she left the back door of her greenhouse unlocked and was asking him to go check but I could tell that he was anxious to get home to her so I told him that I would go check. I wouldn't be caught dead in a shithole place like that and a little thing like you never should have stepped foot in there. What were you thinking, Trixie?"

He turns left and into a gravel parking lot, coming to a stop close to the front of a building. I squint through the rain and make out a sign. Rose's Greenhouse and Nursery.

"Stay here," he orders and I grit my teeth.

I don't like him ordering me around like I'm some annoying little kid. This is something that my mother would have done. If she had caught me at that bar, I never would have heard the end of it. She would have grounded me for the rest of my life.

Maybe it was the way he asked what I was thinking, in that same disappointed tone that I've heard so many times before. It's the same thing that my mother says every time I've gone against something that she ordered. Suddenly, I am so completely done. He was supposed to be different. He was supposed to treat me better than this.

Before I can think better of it, I kick open the passenger door and run out into the rain after him. I saw him duck around the back and I head in that direction, wiping away the rain as it runs in my eyes. There's a light on by the back door and I see Zeke there, huddled under the awning. He's typing something on his phone but he looks up as my feet crunch on the gravel closer to him.

It smells like rain and dirt and I don't know why but that's when I snap.

"You were supposed to be different," I shout.

"What are you doing, Trixie? Get back in the car," he yells back and I can feel tears threatening to form in my eyes.

"You were supposed to be different," I say again and he jogs over to where I'm stopped.

"Different how?" He asks, his voice raising to be heard over the rain.

"You acted like you liked me, like you thought I was smart."

"I do think you're smart."

"You just yelled at me and treated me like a little kid," I say, pointing back to where his SUV is still running in the lot.

"You're not old enough to drink. You shouldn't have been in that place. Bad things could have happened to you," he says, stepping closer to me.

"You're not my dad or my boyfriend or even a friend. You're just a guy. You don't get to tell me what to do and you don't get to treat me like that," I say before I spin on my heel and walk away from him.

Sure, we're about an hour's walk from my dorm but I'd rather walk in the rain then sit through another car ride like that with him. Before I can even make it two steps, a hand is wrapping around my arm and I'm spun around.

"Just some guy? I'm just some guy to you? You're going to stand there and tell me that you don't feel this between us?"

My breath catches and my heartbeat seems to stop. At least the one in my chest seems to stop. A new one, between my legs, roars to life and I whimper, squeezing my thighs tight together to try to ease the ache forming there. Zeke looks down at my legs and smirks and I feel my spine straighten.

"That's not the punishment for lying," I say and part of me wonders what the hell I'm doing.

"No? Well then, what is?"

"Soap in your mouth," I whisper, my voice barely a whisper over the rain thundering down all around us.

"I don't have any soap, but I can think of something else to fill your mouth with," he says a second before his lips slam down on mine.

I moan, my hands wrapping around his neck. I've never been kissed before and I wasn't sure what to expect. A friend of mine in high school had made it sound bad but there's nothing bad about what Zeke is doing to me.

His mouth molds to mine, like he's trying to memorize the shape and feel of it against his but then it's like a switch has been flipped. The slow and teasing kiss of a second ago is gone and now it's hard and hungry. He devours me, licking at the seam and teasing the corner of my lips before he nips my bottom lip.

He coaxes my tongue out to play with his before his hands tangle in my wet hair and he angles my head up, plunging his tongue into my mouth and tangling it sensuously with mine. I can't keep up. I feel dizzy as he continues to claim my mouth. The ache between my legs is worse, so much worse and I whine low in my throat.

I want to climb him, to tug him closer but we're both soaked and my fingers keep slipping. Zeke growls, his hands slipping under my thighs and he lifts me, taking a few steps over to the side of the greenhouse where he pins me between him and the wall.

He grinds his hips against mine and I tear my mouth from his, groaning his name as his mouth moves lower, licking up the water drops along my neck. My hips roll against his, the wet fabric of my shirt and skirt molding to my body. I can feel the seam of his jeans and the hard ridge inside and I want to ask him for something. I'm not sure what and before I can try to put it into words, his phone rings.

His lips pause their exploration of my neck and he freezes like that, the only sound the harsh pants of our breaths and the rain falling around us. Zeke pulls back, his blue eyes as dark as the night around us as he watches me. My tongue darts out, licking across my lips and he groans, his eyes heating once more.

His phone rings again and with a curse, he sets me back on my feet and digs into his pocket to answer it. He eyes me as I lean back against the building, trying to catch my breath and find the strength for my legs to hold me upright once more. I can barely hear him over the rain but I hear him say Atti and I assume it's Atlas calling about the locks.

The magic of the moment seems to be fading, leaving this dark uncertainty. I wrap my arms around myself as Zeke shoves his phone back in his pocket.

"Come on, Trix I'll drive you home."

I nod, walking ahead of him all the way back to the SUV.

9

Z eke

I FINISH TIDYING up my desk, straightening up some designs that I was working on. I barely slept a wink, too worked up from dry humping Trixie against Darcy's greenhouse. I think my lips are still tingling from our make out session last night. We had driven home in silence, the only sound the rain on the SUV as we made our way through the late night traffic.

I had walked her to her room but before I could kiss her goodnight, she had whispered goodnight and disappeared inside. I spent the rest of the night flipping from horny and turned on to confused and worried that I had somehow messed up things with Trixie before they even started.

Someone knocks on my open door and I spin in my chair, smiling when I see Nico standing there. I didn't even hear anyone come in and I check my watch, seeing that we still have about half an hour before the shop opens.

"Hey, Nico. You're in early," I say as I stand.

"Yeah... I wanted to give you a warning," he says, shifting uncomfortably and my stomach drops. No way can this be good.

"What's up?"

"Atlas and Mischa were having a double date last night and it seems that Darcy has security cameras around the greenhouse. Atlas insisted on it a couple of months ago," he says.

"Okay..." I say, my voice trailing off as I try to figure out where he's going with this.

"And Darcy brought it up on her phone because Mischa and Indie are thinking about getting a new security system for their apartment."

I stare blankly at Nico, wondering what the heck is going on with him. He usually gets straight to the point. He's the most no-nonsense person that I've ever met so it's not like him to ramble on like this.

"And they brought up the footage while you were there and Mischa saw you and that Trixie girl making out and he seems pretty excited about it," he finishes in a rush.

I close my eyes in pain, already knowing what's about to happen.

"Hey, Dadddddddd!" Mischa sings out as he bounces into the shop. I hear the metal gate bang shut and I sit back in my chair, holding my head in my hands.

Nico shifts out of the doorway but I notice that he doesn't leave the room. Instead he tucks himself into the corner and crosses his arms over his chest. I glare at him and he shrugs, giving me an unapologetic smile.

"So tell me," Mischa says without preamble when he

comes into my room. "Which article was it that got you to seal the deal? I'm thinking I'll have to send them to Nico here next."

"I didn't read any of the articles," I tell Mischa as he hops up on my tattoo table. Atlas and Sam come into the room after him and Atti jumps up next to him on the table while Sam takes the other chair in the room.

"You didn't miss anything. Those articles were all really vague and none of the information was even useful," Atlas says.

"I'll still send them to you, Nico," Mischa tries to reassure Nico.

"Please don't."

"Well it had to be something!" Mischa says. "How did Zeke get a hot girl like Trixie if not for my articles and guidance?"

"Guidance?" Sam asks with a snort.

"Yeah, we already talked about how I am the love master in this shop," Mischa tells her and I try to sit perfectly still, hoping that they forget about me.

"Do you not remember how you almost lost Indie?" She asks him and he rolls his eyes.

"We told him," Atlas says and Mischa elbows him in the side.

"I didn't lose her and now we're the best couple in the world. Real couple goals," he boasts and I roll my eyes.

"Back to Zeke," Sam says and I throw a glare her way.

"Yeah, so how did you get Trixie to agree to go out with you?" Mischa asks again.

"I didn't. I mean, I haven't asked her out yet."

"Well, why not?" Atlas asks.

"Yeah, if you want advice about asking a girl out then definitely don't ask Mischa. He's the poster child for waiting too long to ask someone out," Sam says and he flips her off over his shoulder.

"That's not- that's not it," I admit and I see I have all of their attention.

"What's the problem? Trixie seemed nice. I know Darcy liked her," Atlas says and I smile, loving that that's all it takes for Atlas to like someone.

"Yeah, what's the problem, Dad? If you want your son's blessing, well then you have it," he says and even though he's joking, I can see that he still means it.

"You don't think she's too young for me?" I ask, finally voicing the one concern that's been in the back of my mind since I met Trixie.

"Who cares about age?" Sam asks and I realize that she's in a similar boat to me.

Max is my age and Sam is just a few years older than Trixie so I guess it really isn't that different then what is happening between Trixie and I.

"Yeah, who cares about age. As long as she makes you happy, then that should be all that matters," Nico agrees.

"Besides, you're so old, Dad. You're probably going to die any day now. You need to make good use of the time you have left. We just want you to be happy in your final years," Mischa says, giving me a pitying look.

I flip him off but it feels like a weight has lifted. I don't really care about what everyone thinks. The only people's opinions I care about are Trixie's and the people in this room. If they're all okay with me dating, and if Trixie wants me, then I'm all in with her.

"I think it makes sense that you'd find someone younger than you. You're so protective. Everyone here looks at you as a big brother... or a dad," he says waving his hand toward Mischa who grins at him. "You're always the guy to take care of others, to take care of us. I'm sure you'll take care of Trixie too."

I nod. I do like taking care of people. I'm used to it. Probably from when I had to take care of my mom when I was a kid. I've always been protective of the people who work here. They've become family to me over the years, the family that I wish I had when I was growing up. Sure, Mischa drives me up the walls and Sam can be mischievous, but I wouldn't trade them for anything.

Mischa claps his hands, pulling me out of my thoughts.

"Now that we've got Zeke matched up, it's your turn!" He says, spinning around on the table and pointing at Nico.

Nico looks like he's regretting staying in the room when they all had gotten here and I give him an unapologetic smile.

"No thanks. I can take care of it myself."

"All you do is work, man. Where are you going to meet a girl?" Mischa asks and Sam and Atlas turn to look at him then too.

"I'll be alright," Nico says and it looks like Mischa wants to argue some more but it's time for us to open.

I hear a knock on the front door and Sam sighs as she goes to answer it.

"Get to work, ya slackers," I say as I stand.

Mischa and Atlas hop off the table and Nico straightens from the wall but none of them leave.

"You should ask her out, Z," Atlas says as he comes over and claps me on the shoulder.

"Yeah, dad. What he said," Mischa says and I step forward before he can react and wrap my arms around him.

"Thanks, son." He squirms in my hold and I hug him tighter. "Come on, Atlas and Nico. Get in here."

Nico and Atti grin as they join me and I laugh when

Atlas yells for Sam to come join us too. She bounces into the room and wraps her arms around us too.

"Why does this keep happening?" Mischa asks with a groan.

"Are we interrupting something?" A soft voice asks and I start, realizing that I forgot we had a customer. I turn to the door and smile when I see Indie, Darcy, and Max all standing there.

"Group hug?" Indie asks and Mischa starts to shake his head no frantically.

They all join us though before he can get away and I laugh as we cram everyone into the room together. Atlas has his arm wrapped around Darcy and Mischa, Sam is smashed between Max and Atlas, Indie is half standing on the tattoo table, half hanging off of Mischa who has his arms wrapped around her in a tight hug, a manic smile on his face. Nico is next to me and he grins as he takes in the scene, hitting his shoulder against mine.

As I take in the scene, I know what I have to do, what I want to do. I need to finally ask Trixie out on a proper date.

10

T rixie

I TRY to turn the volume up on my headphones again but I have a feeling that nothing will be loud enough to drown out the sounds of two of my roommates having sex in the next rooms. It's been happening on and off all day which didn't bother me earlier because I could go to the library but it closed at six and I had to come back to our dorm room.

I've been working on my project all day and I need to finish it this weekend since it's due on Monday. I've been putting it off all week for two reasons. One, I was starting to get behind in some of my business classes and I need to catch up and two, because every time I started to work on my project, I would get lost in thoughts of Zeke.

It's been a whole week since our kiss in the rain and I haven't heard from him. I haven't tried to reach out to him either but that's because I don't know what to say to him. I don't know what he wants and I'm getting sick of his hot and cold routine. One second he's pulling me into him, holding my hand and taking me to his place and the next he's dropping me off without a backward glance.

I know what I want. I want him.

He makes me feel safe and cared for, like I could do anything, be myself, and he would still be there for me. I've never had that before and the feeling is addicting. I love talking art with him, learning from him and looking at some of the pieces and tattoo designs that he's done. I even showed him some of my work the last time I went to the shop. I never show anyone my art but I trust Zeke. He would never put me down like that. He's like the parent, best friend, and boyfriend that I've always dreamed about rolled up into one delectable man.

My roommate moans in the next room, loud enough for me to hear over the rock music blaring from my headphones. I want to bang my head against the wall but instead, I shove everything into my bag and stand. Maybe I can find a coffee shop or something that's still open and finish up my work there.

I sneak out into the living room and I'm about to pull open the front door when there's a knock on it. I jerk it open, praying that it's not my third roommate's date for the night.

My mouth drops open when I see Zeke standing there, a bouquet of roses and a box of chocolates in his hand. He opens his mouth but before he can get a word out, more moans come from my roommates' rooms and has his eyes narrowing.

I grab his arm, slamming the door closed behind me and dragging him down the hall. He takes over after a few steps, tugging my backpack off my shoulder and passing me the flowers before he laces our fingers together. He leads me over to his car and helps me inside, passing me the chocolates and setting my backpack in the backseat before he climbs behind the wheel.

"What's all this for?" I ask, motioning to the flowers and chocolates.

"The articles said..." He trails off and I turn to see him staring straight ahead. If I didn't know any better, I'd say that he was blushing and it makes my lips quirk up.

"Articles?" I ask, fighting a laugh.

"Yeah, never mind and do me a favor and never tell Mischa that I said that."

I giggle and Zeke smiles, turning to look at me before we pull off of campus.

"I missed you and I wanted to come surprise you and see if you wanted to grab dinner with me sometime."

We stop at a red light and I study him.

"Yeah, I'd like that," I say softly and Zeke's shoulders relax as he turns and grins at me.

He reaches over, cupping the back of my head and pulling me closer to him. Our lips meet in a soft kiss and I want to unbuckle and crawl into his lap, but Zeke pulls away.

"Where to?" He asks and I blink back to reality.

"Oh, uh, I was just going to go to a coffee house or something so that I can finish some homework."

"My place alright?" He asks as the light turns green.

"Perfect," I say with a sigh, relaxing back into the seat.

We make small talk on the way to his place and he asks me about my classes and how my project is coming along. It's weird that this guy I just met knows more about me and my life than people who have known me for years.

"Are you hungry?" Zeke asks as we turn onto Main Street.

"Oh, yeah!" I say, sitting up in my seat more as we drive past some restaurants.

"What would you like, Trix?"

"A burger and milkshake," I say, my mouth watering at the thought of a juicy burger and thick milkshake.

Zeke smiles and turns into the lot of a popular burger joint. He parks and is about to shut the SUV off when a loud bang sounds on his window. I jump in my seat and Zeke jerks around, swearing slightly when he sees Mischa standing there laughing.

Then Indie, the purple eyed girl from the shop bounces up next to him and waves at Zeke, her face breaking out into a grin when she sees me in the passenger seat. She starts to race around to my side but trips over something. Mischa catches her, steadying her and planting her back onto her feet. She smacks a kiss on his cheek and he smiles down at her sweetly.

It's obvious these two are in love and I can't help but long for what they have. My eyes find Zeke's and he seems to be having some kind of silent conversation with Mischa through the window. Zeke glares at him and Mischa wiggles his eyebrows back at him, a maniacal smile on his face.

"Are we getting out?" I ask Zeke after they keep staring at each other.

"No," Zeke says at the same time I see Mischa and Indie nodding frantically through the window.

I grin at them before I throw my door open and climb out. I hear Zeke mutter curses under his breath before he climbs out too and joins us in front of the restaurant. His hand goes to my lower back and he sighs loudly before he looks to Mischa.

"Trixie, you remember Mischa and his girlfriend, Indie."

"Yeah, hey guys," I say with a smile.

"Hey," Indie says as she bounces over to me and envelopes me in a hug. It's a good thing that Zeke has a hand on my back because she almost bowls me over.

"We already texted Atlas, Sam, and Nico. They're on their way," Mischa says with a grin and Zeke just tugs me closer.

Just then, two cars pull up and Atlas and Darcy climb out of one car. Nico lumbers out from the other and lifts his hands in a wave. They join us in front of the restaurant as another car pulls up and I smile when I see Sam's bright purple hair. She climbs out and joins a man that looks to be about Zeke's age.

"Trix, you've already met Sam and this is Max. Max, Trixie."

I shake Max's hand, giving Zeke a reassuring smile as we all file into the restaurant.

11

Zeke

DINNER LAST NIGHT went better than I had anticipated after I saw the crazy look on Mischa's face. It was loud, everyone talking over each other, and I had worried that Trixie would feel overwhelmed but she handled it like a pro. Her and the other girls already made plans to do a girls night on Friday, which is why I have to wait until Saturday to take Trixie out on our first official date.

I try not to grumble too much about her going out. I know that she was excited to be making friends and I want her to fit in with my family. She had chatted about them and their plans the whole way back to my place last night. I had helped her with her project as best I could and then she had passed out on the couch. I got to make her breakfast this morning before she had to head out for her Monday classes.

I had headed into work after I dropped her off. I've been in my room for over an hour, working on a tattoo design. Trixie keeps drawing these cherry blossoms everywhere. I had asked about it last night and she admitted that she always loved them. She told me a little about her mom and how controlling she is. My hands clench as I remember how she admitted that she didn't want to go to college for business, how boring she found all of her classes except for her art one.

I had asked her what she wanted to do with her life and she had answered right away. Artist. She wanted to draw and paint and create. I could relate.

She told me that the cherry blossom is a symbol of renewal and the fleeting nature of life. They don't last very long and she was hoping that it would give her the strength and courage to stand up to her mom one day. I'd like to have a chat with her mother myself but I know that Trixie has to be the one to do it.

I've been drawing cherry blossoms for a couple of hours, weaving them into other designs or drawing three bunches together. There's even a whole tree around here somewhere. I finish shading in one design where the blossoms are wrapped around a T. I already know that I'll be getting this tattooed on me soon. There's a matching one with a Z instead of a T in the pile too and my cock hardens to steel in my pants when I think about tattooing it onto Trixie.

I heard the others come into the shop a few minutes ago but everyone is dragging a little after our late night. Suddenly, Mischa appears in the doorway, his eyes wide with shock. He looks flushed and I wonder if he's sick.

"Dad, come quick," he says and my heart rate picks up, kicking hard against my chest.

"What's wrong?" I ask, jerking out of my chair.

"It's Nico," Mischa says, turning and bolting down the hallway.

My stomach drops and I follow him down the hall and behind the front counter and see Sam and Atlas already standing there.

"What's wrong?" I ask, looking around for Nico or the source of panic.

"SHH!" They all say at once and I frown.

"He's *smiling*," Sam says, like she can't believe what she's seeing.

"And texting. He hates texting. Every time I send him a message he messages back saying unsubscribe," Mischa says, a bewildered expression on his face.

I laugh at that. I can only imagine how pissed Mischa is every time he sends Nico a message and gets that back. I file that information away, intending to use it later. We all stare open mouthed at Nico who is sitting in a chair in the lobby, smiling down softly at his phone.

"Who could he possibly be talking too? Everyone he knows is here," Atlas says, chewing on his bottom lip.

"Maybe he's got a girl," I say, remembering how he had been acting weird and asking me about dating a few weeks ago.

"A girl?!?" Mischa says, his outburst causing Nico to look up and see all of us standing there staring at him.

Nico's cheeks turn a rosy red and I have to hold Mischa back when he tries to jump over the counter, presumably to grab Nico's phone and find out for himself.

"You keeping secrets, Nico?" Sam asks, a gleeful look in her eyes as she edges her way toward the gate. Nico shoots a panicked look in my direction but I just shrug back.

"You have a girlfriend?" Mischa asks in disbelief.

"Yeah, and I didn't even need any advice from Eye Candy Ink's resident romance expert," Nico says drily and Mischa laughs.

"When are we going to get to meet her?" I ask, my arms still wrapped around Mischa's shoulders. I can feel how tense he is and I know that if I let him go, he'll be out in the lobby with Sam trying to corner Nico.

"You should have invited her last night," Atlas says, typing away on his phone. I'd bet everything I have that he's telling Darcy about Nico and his girlfriend.

"She's out of town a lot," Nico mumbles, shoving his phone in his pocket and standing up. He eyes Sam warily as she stops a few feet away.

"Ohhhh, I see what's going on here," Mischa says and he relaxes. I loosen my hold on him, leaving one arm draped over his shoulders in case I need to hold him back again.

"What?" Atlas asks, looking up from his phone.

"Nico has a "girlfriend"," Mischa says, using air quotes around the word girlfriend.

Nico rolls his eyes. "She's real."

"Right, she just lives in Canada or something then? Where did you meet? The chat room at CatfishRUs?"

Nico grins at that, chuckling softly. "No, she came in with a client a couple of weeks ago. The night Trixie came in actually."

I try to think back to that night but I couldn't tell you who else was in the shop. I only had eyes for Trixie.

"When do we get to meet her?" I ask but before he can answer, the door flings open and our first customer of the day walks in.

"Morning," Sam says with a fake smile as she heads back around to the counter.

"Alright, everyone back to work," I say as I head back to my room.

"We're not done talking about this," Mischa says, pointing a finger at Nico.

I ignore them all and head back into my room, picking up my pencil and drawing another cherry blossom design.

12

———

T rixie

ZEKE and I have been texting and talking on the phone every day. I know that he was grumpy that he had to wait until the next weekend for us to go out on our date and if I was being honest, I was a little sad to have to wait too. Zeke was making the wait worth it though.

He brought me dinner twice last week and met up with me for lunch one day too. I know his hours at Eye Candy Ink are a little weird but it's more lenient since he's the boss and we were making it work. He texted me sweet things every morning and he was always asking me how my classes were going and if I needed anything.

These were vastly different from the weekly phone calls I got from my mother. In those calls, she only asked how my grades were and if I had looked into any internships for next year. I had never really looked forward to those phone calls from her but now I actively dreaded them.

It's Friday night and I stare at myself in the mirror, looking over my outfit for girl's night. We're just going to Indie and Mischa's place so I'm dressed casually in a plain t-shirt and a pair of black yoga pants. Sam told me to wear something I didn't mind ruining and I didn't really have any old clothes with me. My mother likes for me to be put together at all times and she never lets me buy anything that doesn't look like it could be worn to church. The t-shirt and yoga pants are some that I found on clearance at the mall when I was home for summer break and snuck back to college with me.

I tuck my hair back behind my ears and turn to grab my phone. Indie's place isn't too far from me but it's late and I know that Zeke would freak if he found out that I was walking around at night by myself. Before I can pull up the Uber app, there's a knock at my door and I frown. I really don't want to deal with one of my roommates' boyfriends right now and I steel myself as I pull the door open.

"Zeke! What are you doing here?" I ask when I see him standing there.

"It's girl's night, right?" He asks, wrapping his arms around my waist and dropping a quick kiss on my lips. "I'm here to give you a ride."

"That's sweet of you," I say as I close and lock the door behind us. "I was just going to order an Uber."

Zeke's fingers tighten on my hip as he leads me down the hall and out to his SUV. "I'm not trying to tell you how to live your life, but I'd prefer it if you didn't get into cars with strangers," he says, his voice coming out tense.

I know he wants to order me not to ever use an Uber but he's probably remembering our fight last week when I yelled at him for treating me like a child. I nod my head, resting it against his shoulder as he steers me over to his car.

He kisses me again before he closes the passenger door and I smile. He asks me about my classes and tells me about work and some tattoo designs that he's been working on. I ask to see them and he nods toward a notepad in the back seat. I smile as I flip through it, my hand pausing when I get to the first cherry blossom drawing.

I study it, taking in the clean lines before I flip the page. There's another cherry blossom there and I know that these are because of me, for me. He's drawn my favorite flower, something that means a lot to me, over and over again. I flip through the pages, admiring all of the different designs. I love how creative and talented he is. My hand freezes when I come to the matching T and Z designs and my heart kicks in my chest.

A T for Trixie and a Z for Zeke. This has to mean something. He hasn't said the words but all of those cherry blossoms and then this, it has to mean that he loves me. Right? Why else would he do it otherwise? Why else would he be designing a tattoo like this? It's so... permanent.

"I'll walk you up," Zeke says as he shuts the SUV off and I realize that we must be at Indie's place already.

I take one last look at the design as Zeke comes around to open my door.

"I want this," I tell him, pointing at the Z.

Zeke's eyes heat and he nods. "I'll do it for you," he whispers as he closes the notepad and kisses me slowly.

"Gross, boss," I hear and we break apart.

Sam and Max are standing on the sidewalk with their arms wrapped around each other. Max is grinning at Zeke and Sam gives me a soft smile, twirling a plastic bag around her finger. Max has a couple of paper bags in his hands and my mouth waters at the smell that is coming out of them.

"I see you couldn't ditch your man either. So much for girls night, huh?" Sam asks as she steps away from Max and wraps her arm around mine, leading me into the building.

Zeke and Max trail after us and we ride up to the third floor in the elevator. A door is already open and I see Indie poke her head out when she hears the elevator ding.

"They're here! Get out!" She yells, disappearing back into the apartment.

A second later, a grumbling Atlas and Mischa are pushed out into the hallway. Atlas cradles Darcy's face in his hands, kissing her almost reverently and I smile. I grin wider, when Mischa grabs Indie's hand, twirling her once and tugging her into him. That familiar half wild, half-crazy grin is on his face although it softens when she laughs up at him. He kisses her, slipping his tongue in her mouth and I turn away from the sight.

Max is kissing Sam goodbye and she gives him a wicked grin as she slips away from him with the food in her other hand. He just laughs at her and I turn to look at Zeke. His eyes are locked on me and I gulp when I see the depth of emotion in them. He steps into me, his thumbs stroking over my cheeks as he tips my head up. His lips meet mine and I open my mouth immediately, desperate for him, for his taste.

"Come on! I'm starving. See you later, boys," Sam calls, hooking her arm through mine and dragging me away from Zeke.

He licks his lips, giving me a heated look before he nods slightly.

"I'll be downstairs at Atlas's place," he tells me and I nod right as Sam slams the door shut behind us.

"Did you get everything?" Darcy asks Sam as she takes a seat at the kitchen counter.

"Yep," Sam says cheerfully, dumping her bag out as Indie takes out all of the food.

Boxes of hair dye spill out onto the counter and my eyes widen when I see a pale pink. My mother would never allow me to dye my hair but the longer I stare at the pink box, the more I want to do it. I'm already making Zeke give me a tattoo, might as well go for broke. Besides, my mother never comes to visit me so I know I can have it back to my normal platinum blonde before I see her again.

"We're dying our hair tonight?" I ask and Indie nods.

"Sam is the master at it and she said she'd help us. You don't have to if you don't want to," she tells me and I know that she means it.

These girls would never try to make me do something that I didn't want to and my mind flashes back to the one night I spent out with my roommates, when they tried to get me to drink and do shots with them, even after I told them I didn't want to.

"I want to," I say shyly and they all grin at me.

I'm passed a plate and we all stand, loading up on burgers and French fries, mozzarella sticks and so much more. Indie explains that Sam's boyfriend owns restaurants so she has the best hookups. We eat around the kitchen counter, all of us stuffing our faces as we laugh and get to know each other more.

I offer to help clean up but Indie waves me off and next thing I know, we're all crowded into her bathroom, boxes of hair dye littering every spare surface.

"Did you just go to the store and get one of every color?" Darcy asks as she eyes all of them.

"No, Max comes home with a few new boxes every week."

My heart melts at that and I can see the dreamy look in her eyes when she talks about him. Indie grabs a box of purple hair dye and starts to ask Sam about it. Her hair is so dark that she'd have to bleach it for any color to show up and Indie pouts for a minute. She recovers quickly, smiling happily as she helps Darcy pick out a color. Sam comes over to me, shaking the box of pink dye that I had been eyeing in the kitchen.

I spend the next hour getting high on fumes and giggling so much that my stomach hurts. The bathroom is small and we keep bumping into each other but no one seems to mind. By the end, my hair is a gorgeous pastel pink color. I love it and I can't stop running my fingers through it. Sam warned me that it would wash out fast and Indie immediately piped up and said we'd just have another girls night when it did.

There's a knock at the door and Indie walks over to open it, throwing herself at Mischa as soon as she sees him.

"Sam's going to give me a piercing," she tells him and I vaguely remember them discussing it earlier.

"Is that so?"

"Yep! Right now, if that's alright with you, Zeke," Indie says and Zeke tears his eyes away from me.

"Yeah that's fine. Trix wanted some ink done too. We can all go."

"Girls night continues!" Indie cheers and I grin at her as Mischa carries her out of the apartment.

Atlas wraps his arm around Darcy, telling her how much he likes the purple tips of her hair and she beams up at him. Max smiles at Sam, tugging on the ends of her dark blue hair. Zeke and I are last and he tugs me into his side, making sure the door is locked behind us before we follow them down the hall.

"You look beautiful," he says and I grin, tipping my face up to meet his eyes.

"Thanks. I love it."

"Me too," he whispers as he helps me into the car.

We make the short drive over to Eye Candy Ink and Zeke helps me out of the SUV before he unlocks the front door. I follow him back into his room as the others wander around the shop.

"Are you sure about this?" Zeke asks, flipping to the cherry blossom tattoo. "You can think about it a bit if you want."

"I'm sure," I tell him and he grins at me, leaning in to kiss me quickly before he starts pulling out supplies.

I know that it might be too soon to get his initial tattooed on me but time doesn't matter to me with this. This is the first thing that I'm choosing for myself. Zeke is the first person that I've chosen to be in my life. Everything else, everyone else, my mother has decided for me. Even if Zeke and I don't work out, which would break my heart, at least I would always have this reminder that I need to be stronger and make my own decisions in my life.

Max, Atlas, and Darcy come into our room to see what's going on and they all admire the design as Zeke finishes setting up. He kicks them out when he's ready and they head back to see how Sam and Indie are doing.

"Where do you want it, Trix?" Zeke asks me.

"Here," I say, pointing to my left side. That way it will be over my ribs so I'll be able to hide it from my mother easily and next to my heart, so I'll always remember the first man I ever loved.

Zeke instructs me to take my shirt off and he gives me an

Eye Candy Ink shirt so that I can cover myself up a little bit. If I wasn't in love with him before, I would have fallen for him after that. He lays out the tattoo against my skin and shows it to me to approve and then he gets to work.

I try to watch him the best I can. It helps me ignore the sting from the needle as he moves along my skin. He rubs the excess ink away as he continues to outline the cherry blossoms. The Z curves along my ribs, the cherry blossoms tucked behind it and wrapping around the middle.

I'm not aware of time as I watch Zeke work. He's so confident, so talented and I'm in awe of him when he finally shows me the finished product an hour and a half later.

"It's beautiful, Zeke," I tell him and he smiles at me as he bandages it up.

"Now, it's my turn," he says and my mouth waters when he reaches behind his neck and tugs his shirt off.

I avert my eyes so that I don't start drooling and gingerly pull the Eye Candy Ink shirt over my head. Zeke's door opens and Indie sticks her head in.

"Is it done? Can I see it?" She asks when she sees me dressed.

Zeke shows her the drawing pad design and I grin when Indie gushes over it.

"What are you doing, dad?" Mischa asks, coming up behind Indie.

Atlas, Sam, and Max all crowd in after them and Zeke rolls his eyes.

"I'm getting a tattoo," he says calmly, flipping the page to the matching T cherry blossom design.

"Matching tattoos?!?" Indie yells, bouncing up and down on her feet. "Oh, that is so cute!"

"It's also the kiss of death for relationships," Mischa mumbles and Atlas elbows him in the ribs.

"I have Darcy's name tattooed on me," he reminds him and I hear Zeke chuckle next to me.

"Are you saying you wouldn't get my name tattooed on you, Mischy?"

"Mischy?!?" Sam and Atlas say with glee.

"No," he says, pointing a finger at them.

"Zeke, could you draw us matching tattoos too?" Indie asks, wrapping her arm around Mischa.

"I'll be the one drawing our tattoos," Mischa grumbles and she beams up at him.

"Make it something pretty."

Sam chuckles at that and Mischa just rolls his eyes.

"Yeah, yeah," he mumbles, stooping down to kiss her.

"You want me to do the tattoo?" Atlas offers but Zeke shakes his head.

"Trix is going to do it," he says and my mouth drops open.

"What?" I ask, wondering if he's lost his mind.

"I trust you," he tells me with a smile as he lays out the supplies.

"Mischa and Atlas can supervise if you want," he tells me as he leads me over to the chair and hands me a pair of latex gloves.

My hands are shaking as I pull the gloves on but I can't tell if it's from nerves or excitement. Atlas and Mischa stand behind me, explaining what to do next and Darcy, Sam, Max, and Indie all crowd in the doorway, watching as I learn how to tattoo.

It takes me far longer than it did Zeke and my lines aren't as clean as the ones he did on me, but at the end of it, Zeke has a matching tattoo to mine. Zeke's is on his side too and he grins down at it before he grabs some bandages and covers it up. He tugs his shirt back on and kisses me, licking along the seam of my lips before he pulls away from me.

It's well after midnight and I yawn as Zeke closes up the shop and walks me out to his SUV. We wave goodbye to the others as they all climb into their cars and we head off in different directions.

"You alright staying at my place tonight, Trix?" He asks as he starts up his SUV.

"Yeah, that sounds perfect," I say with a sigh as I lean my head against the passenger door. I think I'm asleep before we even make it a block.

13

Z eke

I LET Trixie sleep in the next morning. I know that she must be tired after how late we were up last night. When she still isn't awake by ten, I text Nico and let him know that I won't be in for a bit. I don't want to leave Trixie here by herself without a car or anything. I need to go grocery shopping too and I peek into the fridge, sighing when I see that I don't even have eggs or milk for breakfast.

I'm debating if I should run out for some takeout when I hear Trixie start to wake up. I make my way over to where she is tucked up in the bed. She fell asleep there last night so I slept on the couch. I perch on the edge of the bed, smoothing some of Trixie's freshly dyed locks away from her face. She gives me a sleepy smile, pulling herself up to sitting and leaning against the headboard.

"Morning, sleepyhead," I say with a smile and she smiles

sweetly back at me, her eyes starting to perk up more as she wakes up.

"Morning. What time is it?" She asks, looking around.

"About 10:30 am."

"What!" She asks, her eyes wide.

"What's wrong?" I ask with a frown, wondering if she had some class or meeting to get to that I was unaware of.

"It's just, I've never slept that late in my life."

She looks so grumpy and upset about it that I can't help but laugh. I drop a kiss on her nose before I stand up.

"I was going to run out and grab some breakfast. Want me to bring you back something or would you like to come with me? Or I can drop you off at your dorm if you have something else you need to do."

"I'll come with you," she says, tossing back the covers and sliding out of bed. "Just give me ten minutes to get ready."

"Take your time," I tell her as she heads for the bathroom.

I tidy up my apartment, folding up the blankets from the couch and stuffing them and the pillows back in the closet. I'm just closing the door when Trixie steps out of the bathroom. She's wearing the black Eye Candy Ink shirt that I gave her last night and I decide that I need to get her one in every color.

"How's the tattoo?" I ask as we walk down to the SUV.

"Good, a little itchy," she says as I help her inside the SUV.

"That's normal," I reassure her and she nods.

We decide on McDonald's breakfast and we laugh about last night over hash browns and iced coffees. She tells me about what the girls did last night and I can tell that she loves Indie, Darcy, and Sam already. She asks me what the guys did and I tell her we just went down to Atlas's place and hung out.

We head to the grocery store after breakfast and I load up on some of the essentials along with everything that Trixie so much as looks twice at. She looks like she's drooling when we pass the steak section and I make a spur of the moment decision.

"I made reservations for us tonight but would you rather stay in? We can get some steaks and grill at our place."

"Really? You don't mind? It's just been so long since I've had a home cooked meal."

"We can do whatever you want, Trix," I tell her, glad that she didn't seem to catch my slip about *our* place.

We load up on steaks, potatoes, and some cupcakes for dessert before we push the overflowing cart up to the front and checkout. Trixie asks if we can run by the dorm so she can grab a change of clothes and I head in that direction, walking inside with her and carrying her bag back out to the car. We drop the groceries off at home and Trixie tells me she has some homework to do so I leave her to it, heading to the shop to see how things are running there.

It's Saturday so everyone is working and they're all busy with clients. I don't stay long, just a few minutes so I can finish up payroll and some other paperwork and then I'm heading home to my girl.

She's got headphones in and is bent over the counter, scribbling on a piece of paper. I don't want to disturb her so I grab some spray paint and head back downstairs. I'm halfway through the cherry blossom tree when Trixie comes down the stairs and finds me. She smiles at the tree and I lean over and kiss her before I pull my mask back up.

I find her another mask and her own cans of spray paint and she walks a few feet away to an empty section of wall, frowning as she slips her mask on and starts to shake a can of spray paint. I go back to my own section of wall, grabbing the pink paint and finishing the cherry blossoms.

I finish an hour later and step back to take in the final product. It's damn near perfect and I grin. I'm getting really good at drawing cherry blossoms. I put my paint away and step over to where Trixie is still working. She's drawn the Eye Candy Ink logo and I smile when I see it. There's spots where the paint ran but she caught on quickly and by the time she got to the portraits of my family underneath, she's got it down pat.

I smile when I see the crazy grin on Mischa's face. Indie is next to him with an equally manic smile on her face. She's holding hands with Darcy who has her usual sweet smile on her face. Atlas is next to her, his head tipped down as he smiles at Darcy. Sam and Max are next to them, both of them with little smirks on their faces. Next is us and my heart thumps in my chest at how permanent it seems to be to have her painted on my wall. I'm taller than everyone else, my hair wavy and hanging down to my chin. Trixie is tucked into my side, her hair painted a pale pink in the drawing and I have a feeling that the pink hair is here to stay for a while. Not that I mind. I just want Trixie to be happy. Nico is next to me and I smile when I wonder when we'll be painting his girl next to him.

"You're so fucking talented," I murmur as she steps back into me and I wrap my hand around her waist.

"Thanks," she says and when I spin her around I can see the blush staining her cheeks over her mask.

"You should be at art school. Or screw that, just start painting or drawing or something."

"I kind of liked tattooing you last night actually," she says shyly and I tip her chin up so that she meets my eyes.

"Want me to teach you? You can be my apprentice," I offer and I'm surprised when she nods so quickly.

She helps me clean up the paint, tucking it underneath the stairs and then I take her hand in mine and lead her back upstairs. I let her take a shower first while I get the steaks and everything for dinner out. I didn't realize how late it had gotten as we were painting and my stomach growls as I season the steaks and set them aside.

I wrap the potatoes in aluminum foil and stick them in the oven to bake as Trixie comes out of the bathroom, her hair wrapped up in a towel. She's wearing one of my Eye Candy Ink shirts and a pair of yoga pants that mold to her legs and ass and has me drooling.

I hurry into the shower, scrubbing at my body and trying to get my cock under control as I rinse off. I dress in a pair of loose jeans and my own Eye Candy Ink shirt as I head out of the bathroom and back into the kitchen.

Trixie has a cupcake halfway to her mouth when I walk in and she gives me a guilty look before she pops it in her mouth. I laugh and walk over to her, gripping her hips and lifting her onto the counter. I step between her legs, leaning down and licking some frosting off her lips. She moans against my lips and I use the opportunity to lick into her mouth, teasing her tongue with mine.

The oven timer beeps and I reluctantly pull away. Trixie tries to follow after me and I kiss her once more quickly.

"Let me feed you, Trix," I whisper against her lips and she pouts but lets me go.

She sits on the counter and watches me as I move around, pulling out the indoor grill and throwing the steaks on it. I pass Trixie another cupcake and she beams at me, taking a bite as I hold it out to her. I finish off the cupcake and then suck in a shocked breath when Trixie reaches out and grabs hold of my hand, bringing it to her mouth and licking a stray bit of frosting off of my finger.

I can't hold back the moan that tears up my throat and soon I've got Trixie pinned beneath me on the counter. Her legs wrap around my waist and my fingers tangle in her hair as I practically maul her on the kitchen counter. I hear a beeping in the back of my mind but I can't seem to pull my thoughts together long enough to figure out where it's coming from.

I kiss down Trixie's neck, pulling the collar of her shirt away so that I can nip at her shoulder. The beeping continues but with Trixie grinding against me, the heat of her pussy searing through my jeans, I can't be bothered with it.

"Feed me, Zeke," Trixie says as I kiss my way back to her lips.

Fuck, I would love to feed her something, slip my cock down her throat and fill her tiny mouth with me.

Then it occurs to me what the beeping is and I pull away from Trixie, helping her sit up before I hurry over and flip the steaks, pulling the potatoes out of the oven. Trixie watches me, her eyes dark with lust and I reach down, adjusting myself in my pants as I pull some plates out of the cabinet.

She helps me set the places at the counter and a few minutes later, we're both sitting down to eat. Trixie moans and compliments me on my cooking as we clear our plates. I slide the cupcakes over to us after we're done and she grins at me before she takes a large bite. She's adorable and I want nothing more than to pull her into my lap and devour her but I don't want to push her before she's ready.

Trixie helps me with the dishes and clean up and soon

the kitchen is spotless. I tug Trixie into my arms and she wraps her arms around my waist.

"Want to watch some TV?" I ask her and she slowly shakes her head, a sly grin creeping over her face.

"Want more cupcakes?" I try again and she gives me the slow head shake again as she takes a step back toward the bed.

Her fingers toy with the hem of her shirt as she backs up another step and my mouth waters as I start to follow after her.

"What do you want, Trix?" I ask, my voice coming out low and filled with heat.

"You. Just you."

14

————

T rixie

I DON'T KNOW what has me being so bold but I think that it's just because Zeke makes me feel so comfortable. So comfortable and sexy. My mind flashes back to how he had laid me out before dinner, his lips claiming mine. I had been so hot that it felt like I was burning up for him.

I take a deep breath and tug my shirt up and over my head, standing before him in my lacy bralette and yoga pants. Zeke's eyes heat and he stalks forward, picking me up in his arms and carrying me over to the bed.

"Are you sure about this, Trix?" He asks as he lays me out on the bed and hovers over me.

"Yes. I want you, Zeke."

Zeke is on me then, his hands pulling at my pants as he pushes me into the mattress. He gets my yoga pants and panties down my legs and I blush when he sees how wet he's made me.

"Fuck, Trix. Is this all for me?" He asks, running a finger through my drenched folds.

My back arches off the bed and I moan as he does it again.

"Yes, Zeke!" I cry out and I almost scream when he leans forward and buries his face in my pussy.

I moan as his large hands grip my ass and he holds me there as he lowers his mouth back to my core. His tongue dips out, licking up my center and nudging my clit. He continues the same path over and over again and his tongue is relentless. My legs tremble, my back bowing as he licks and nips his way over my folds. When he has me sopping and on the verge of begging him to fuck me, he sucks my clit into his mouth and flicks the sensitive nub with the tip of his tongue.

I fall over the edge, crying out as he wrings every ounce of pleasure out of my body. I collapse back against the mattress and I smile drunkenly when I feel Zeke kissing my inner thighs and up my stomach.

His fingers edge under the lace of the bralette and he tugs it off of me. My eyes blink open and I watch as he takes his shirt off, throwing it over the side of the bed. He comes back over me, plumping up one of my breasts with his fingers before he captures a nipple between his lips and sucks hard.

"So perfect," he murmurs against my skin as he switches to the other.

"You don't think they're too small," I ask and he shakes his head, smoothing over the tip with his lips.

He sucks my nipple into his mouth, swirling his tongue around the stiff bud before he nips it gently with his teeth.

"Zeke!" I cry out as I arch my back, trying to get him to take more of me into his mouth.

My head thrashes on the pillow as Zeke switches back and forth between one stiff peak and the other. I didn't know that people could come just from having someone play with their nipples but I'm so close right now that I think one more strong suck and I'll go flying over the edge.

"Zeke," I beg and I don't even know what I'm begging for.

"Don't worry, Trix. I'm gonna take care of you," he says as he kneels on the edge of the bed and shucks his jeans and underwear off.

He's back between my legs a second later, spreading my thighs wide before he settles between them.

"Ready, Trix?" He asks as he looks up at me and I nod frantically.

I've been teetering on the edge for what feels like weeks and I moan as he brushes the tip of his cock between my pussy lips. He pushes inside of me, stretching me wide but I'm so horny and soaking wet that I barely register the sting of pain as he takes my cherry. He pauses when he bottoms out inside of me and I groan, wiggling under him as I start to mewl.

"Zeke, please!" I cry out and Zeke grins at me.

"No need to beg, Trix. I'm going to have you coming so hard that you'll see stars," he promises and my whole body starts to shake as he starts to move.

He pulls back and then surges back inside of me, thrusting hard as he picks up a punishing rhythm. Each drive of his cock inside me has me flying higher and higher toward oblivion.

He reaches between us and his fingers slip over my clit.

My pussy tightens, spasming around his length and Zeke growls.

"Fuck, Trix. You're so goddamn tight and perfect," he grits out against my skin as his pace grows erratic.

My clit pulses and I scream as I go flying over the edge, coming so hard that I really do see stars.

"Trix... Fuck... I love you," Zeke chokes out and I feel his cock jerk inside me as he starts to come.

"I love you too, Zeke," I whisper in his ear and he groans.

I can feel his come leaking out of me before he even pulls out and I realize that we didn't use protection. I probably should have told him that I wasn't on anything and my body flushes as he pants down at me.

"We didn't... I'm not on...anything," I stammer out and Zeke leans down and kisses me.

"Don't worry, Trix. I will always take care of you."

15

Zeke

I WAKE up to the sound of Trixie's cell phone going off in her bag. I blink my eyes, looking over at my alarm clock to see that it's only eight in the morning. Trixie stretches next to me, her little body pressing more firmly against mine and for a second I forget all about her phone.

She blinks her eyes open, smiling shyly at me as I run my hands over her hips and up to cup her perky tits.

"Morning," she says on a moan and I grin wolfishly down at her.

"Morning," I say before my lips land on hers.

She wraps her arms around my neck, tangling her fingers in her hair and I grin as her hips start to rock against mine. My cock slides through her slick folds and she moans as the underside of my dick, where my piercing in, rubs against her clit.

"That feels so good," she says on a breathy whisper and I grin against her shoulder.

"It's the barbell of my piercing," I tell her and she stiffens.

"You're pierced?"

"Yeah, you didn't notice it last night?" I ask, leaning up to look down at her.

"I-I mean you were my first. I just knew that it felt good, really good."

I grin down at her, rubbing the piercing back and forth over her clit until her eyes fall closed and her breaths start to come out in pants.

"Please... please, Zeke," she says, opening her eyes and giving me a pleading look.

I love that she can say that so readily now and I reward her by tucking the tip of my cock inside her opening.

"Are you sore?" I ask as I push forward slightly, watching her face for any sign of pain.

She winces slightly and I pull back, kissing her lips once before I slip under the covers and between her legs. She tries to grab me, her fingers digging into my shoulders and I flip the covers back so I can give her a hard stare.

"You're sore, Trix. Let me take care of you a different way."

"I'm fine. It didn't hurt that much," she protests, still trying to pull me up.

"I never want you to hurt at all," I tell her, staring straight into her eyes so she can see how serious I am.

Her eyes start to water and she blinks rapidly.

"Shit," I mumble, scrambling to sit up and pull her into my lap.

I run my hands over her back, up and down as I try to

soothe her. I'm not sure what I said that made her upset but I promise to find out and then never say it ever again.

"What's wrong, Trix? Tell me and I'll fix it."

"I love you," she says, turning her wet eyes up to meet mine.

"I love you too, but why is that making you cry?"

"I just never thought I'd have something like this," she says, burying her face in my neck.

I let her cry into my shoulder for a few minutes as I continue to stroke her back, trying to comfort her. When she's finally calmed down, I tangle my fingers in her hair, pulling until she tips her head back and meets my eyes.

"I love you, Trix. I'm not going anywhere. I promise."

She tilts her face up more, offering me her mouth and before I can stop her, she sinks down on my length. I growl into her mouth and she smiles against my lips. My hands grip her hips, helping to raise and lower her on my cock until she's found her rhythm.

My hands move up and I palm her small tits, plumping them with my fingers before I lower my mouth and suck one rosy tip into my mouth.

"Zeke!" Trixie cries out as I swirl my tongue around the bud.

Her hips slam down harder and I moan, scraping my teeth over her nipple before I switch to the other one. Trixie arches her back, her pace growing frantic as I continue to switch between her tits. I can feel my balls tighten up more with every pass of her snug pussy along my cock and as her cries get louder and more desperate, the familiar tingles start at the base of my spine.

I know I'm close to coming but I need Trix to get there first so I drop one of my hands, snaking it between us until I find that bundle of nerves between her thighs. My thumb strums it, once, twice, a third time, and then she's falling apart in my arms.

"Zeke!" She cries out hoarsely as her pussy walls spasm along my cock.

She's so fucking tight and her walls are massaging my dick so good that I have no choice but to empty my balls inside of her. I can feel some of my come leaking out of her as I hold her against my chest while she catches her breath. It occurs to me that we didn't use protection again but instead of fear or regret, I only feel happy. Trix is the one for me. I'm sure of it.

She rests her chin on my chest, staring up at me with a smile and I lean down to kiss her when her phone starts ringing again. With a sigh, I help her off the bed and watch as she walks over to answer it. I'm thinking we could take a quick shower together and then I can make her breakfast and I'm about to text Nico and let him know that I'll be in later when I see all of the color drain out of Trixie's face.

I'm out of bed and across the room to her in an instant. I wrap my arms around her and she sways back against me. I can hear some yelling from the other end of the call and I'm about to grab the phone from Trixie and tell whoever is speaking to her like that to fuck off when the yelling cuts off and Trixie lowers the phone.

"That was my mother," she whispers, still staring down at her phone and I want to smash it. "She's on campus looking for me."

16

T rixie

MY PALMS IS clammy in Zeke's as he drives us back to campus. He keeps shooting me nervous looks and then he turns away with a scowl. I have a feeling that he wants to tear my mother apart but I can't afford for him to do that. She's the only family I have and I could never afford college without her.

Zeke parks outside of my dorm building and jumps out, rounding the hood and coming around to my side. I swallow hard as he opens my door and he leans in and unbuckles me.

"I think I should talk to her by myself," I say, clearing my throat when he looks up at me with a stormy look on his face.

"Like hell. You're mine, Trix. I'm coming with you."

"Just... let me do the talking," I say as I slip out of his car and turn to face my building.

I can see my mother from here, already stalking our way. Her eyes flare when she sees the way Zeke has his arm wrapped around my waist, his hold possessive. He glares right back at her and I sigh, already knowing this isn't going to go well.

"Let me do the talking," I remind him and I try to step away from him but he tightens his grip, keeping me in place as my mother stalks closer.

"Where have you been, Trixie Ann? What did you do to your hair and who is this?" She asks, eyeing my new pink locks and then Zeke with disdain.

"Mom, this is Zeke. Zeke, this is my mother, Rosalie Clemonte."

"Ms. Clemonte," Zeke says politely but I can hear the strain in his voice. He's trying to be nice but he wants to yell at her.

"Where have you been?" My mother asks, ignoring Zeke.

"I was with Zeke," I admit and I feel Zeke curl himself around me even more.

"I see," my mother says, her voice flat and disapproving. "I'd like a word with you. Alone," she says, giving Zeke a withering look. He doesn't even flinch.

"No," he says, his voice deadly.

"Excuse me?" she shrieks and I wince.

"No, I'm not letting Trix go off with you when you're like this."

"Trix?" My mother asks, sneering at him and he glares back at her.

"What are you doing here, mom?" I ask, trying to break the tension.

"I got a call from school about your art project," the way

she says the word art has my heart breaking and I take a step back into Zeke.

"Oh."

"Yes, imagine my surprise when I learned that my daughter had lied and was wasting her time and my money on *art* classes."

"It's not a waste of her time or money," Zeke says. "Trixie is incredibly talented, a natural artist and she's wasted at this school."

"That's none of your concern," My mom says with any icy glare at Zeke.

I don't know if it's just that I've had enough and I'm sick of her criticizing my passion for art or if it's the way that she's treating Zeke, but suddenly I've had enough. I didn't have anyone else in my corner before but now I do. I know that Zeke will always be there for me and I have a feeling having Zeke for family means that I have Atlas, Darcy, Mischa, Indie, Sam, Max, and Nico in my corner as well.

"Stop!" I say, my voice coming out louder than I had intended and my mother rocks back on her heels, staring at me with wide eyes.

She recovers quickly and takes a step toward me which has Zeke moving to step in her path.

"I've got this," I tell him and he takes one look at my face and smiles, crossing his arms across his chest and grinning at me as I turn back to face my mother.

"You have never supported me, mother. You want me to follow your dreams instead of my own and I'm realizing that even if I do stuff my passions down to do as you order, it still won't make you happy."

My mother watches me, her eyes icy and assessing.

"I don't want to go to Carnegie. I don't want to go into business. I love art and I want to be an artist."

"I'm not paying for that," my mother says through gritted teeth.

"I know. I'll get a job."

My mother snorts at that and I feel Zeke tense next to me.

"I'll get a job and I'll work and do art and I'll be happy. I'll be happy because I have Zeke and a whole new family that loves me and only wants me to be happy and I know that they'll support me no matter what," I say, tipping my chin up when she scoffs.

"You think this, this man, is going to be with you for the long run? When your art doesn't sell and times get tough, do you really think that he's still going to be there?"

"Yes," I say honestly and I know that it's true. "I'm sorry that dad left you, mom, but Zeke isn't like that. He loves me and I love him."

"We'll see about that," she says before she turns on her heel and stalks over to her car. I watch her get in and drive off and I know that she'll have my dorm room and class funding pulled before the end of the day.

"Think I can crash with you?" I ask, turning and stepping into Zeke's open arms.

"I was trying to figure out a way to ask you to move in with me so, yes, of course you can, Trix."

I wrap my arms around him and bury my face in his chest, breathing in his comforting scent as I take a moment to figure out how I'm feeling. Zeke holds me, running his fingers through my hair. When I finally pull back and look up at him, he's watching me carefully.

"You alright?" He murmurs and I nod.

"I didn't know if I would be, but yeah, I'm alright. You and everyone else at Eye Candy Ink have already shown me more support and love than she has in the last twenty years. I think I'm going to be just fine without her."

"Hell yeah, you are, Trix. I've got enough money to support us and you can decide for yourself what you want to do. If you want to tattoo, then you know I'll teach you. If you want to paint, then we'll find you a studio and I'll help you any way I can. If you want to go to art school then I'll move to Chicago or wherever with you and I'll pay for it."

"I don't deserve you," I whisper, blinking back tears as I stare up into his blue eyes.

"You're the best thing that ever happened to me, Trix. I love you," he says, leaning down and claiming my lips with his.

He bundles me back into the SUV and I smile as he slips behind the wheel. I know no matter what, I'm going to be safe and loved for the rest of my life.

17

Z eke

I SMILE as Trixie cuddles into my side. We're all crowded into the lobby of Eye Candy Ink as we watch Sam and Max get hitched. You can barely move with all of the flowers that Darcy and Atlas brought in and I keep knocking into a bouquet of some purple flowery thing. I can't remember what it's called but I was told she chose it because of Sam's hair color when they got engaged.

Indie bounces over to Trixie, grabbing her up in a hug before she pulls back and asks to see Trixie's room. She started apprenticing for me right after her mother left and I moved her into my room officially a few days ago. I was barely using it since I've been focused more on the business side of things for awhile.

Trixie isn't quite ready to be on her own yet but she's a fast learner and someone is always here if she has questions. Mischa and Atlas both love helping her because then they can argue over who is the better teacher. Mischa is already trying to take credit for how good Trix is by saying that he taught her everything she knows. Trixie just rolls her eyes at them.

My heart clenches every time I see her interacting with my family. I'm so glad that they all get along and that everyone welcomed her with open arms. This is the family that she needs, the one she deserved all along.

We haven't heard from her mother in months and I don't anticipate that changing. Trixie seems sad about it sometimes but I think she knows that if she goes back, her mother will just try to convince her to change her life all over again.

I've told her some more about my family and life back in Las Vegas and I think that she sees now why I'm always against going back to her. Sure, my mom was an alcoholic but at the end of the day, it boils down to the same thing. They were selfish parents who put their own wants before their children's.

I watch Indie drag Trix away and my breath catches as she stumbles over someone's foot. Nico catches her and steadies her before he turns back to me. I don't know how, but I'd swear that he already knows that Trixie is pregnant. We only found out a week ago but he's been so careful around her for the last few days. He keeps bringing her ginger ale and tea and I keep finding boxes of saltine crackers in the room.

I can still remember the night I came home to find Trix practically bouncing on the couch.

"What's up, Trix?" I asked as I sat down next to her.

"I'm pregnant," she said as she crawled into my lap and nuzzled my neck.

My body tensed as the biggest smile stretched across my lips.

"Really?"

"Yeah, you're going to be a daddy," she said with a laugh before I crushed her against me.

"You're not mad?" she had asked after I had stopped kissing her.

"Why would I be mad?"

"It's just, I know it's so soon and we haven't known each other for very long."

"Trix, if you ever left, there'd never be anyone after you."

I had only asked her to marry me a week and a half before that but still, I don't know how she could doubt that I didn't want everything with her.

We didn't want to take away from Sam and Max's big day so we're waiting until they're back from their honeymoon to tell everyone. Keeping it in is killing me. I want everyone to know that Trix belongs with me but she refused to put the ring on her finger until after Sam and Max were married. She's been wearing it around her neck instead, although I do make her put it on when I fuck her. I love seeing it sparkle on her finger as I pound into her and she claws at my chest.

We've started looking for a new place, one with more room for our kids. It's probably time that I ditched the bachelor pad anyway and it's been fun trying to find a new place that we both like. Trixie thinks that we should keep the warehouse place so we can sneak away when the kids are at school and have somewhere private. She said we can also use it as a studio but the first reason sounds more appealing to me.

Nico sidles over to me as we watch the happy couple up at the front. They've already cut the cake and eaten and I know the party is starting to wind down.

"Congratulations," he says after a minute and I look at him out of the corner of my eye.

"How did you know?" I ask him as I see Trixie and Indie come back out.

Trixie starts to make her way back over to me as Nico clears his throat.

"Because my girl is pregnant too."

18

T rixie

FIVE YEARS LATER...

I NEVER THOUGHT that Zeke would be the stay at home dad type but he's slipped into the role perfectly. I guess I shouldn't be surprised. He's been the dad of the shop for so long and I knew that he would be the best father to our kids.

We had our first baby, a girl we named Nicole, six months after we got married. Our second daughter, Maxine, was born a year after that. Two was more than enough for us especially with both of them born so close together. Zeke cut back his hours at the shop and by then, I was able to tattoo by myself. I've become a pro in the last five years and Zeke and I both like to tease Mischa about how I'm the best in the shop.

I pull up outside our two-story Victorian house and smile when I see Zeke and our girls wave from the front window. We bought this house right after we got married. The warehouse place just wasn't big enough for our expanding family, although we still own it and like to slip away there on date nights or if I can get a break between clients and the girls are still at preschool. I wave as Nico pulls up behind me in his big jeep and he gives me an easy smile as he climbs out. He just got off too and he's here to pick up his son, Zeke. He and his wife decided on that name after Zeke helped deliver him.

Little Zeke runs out of the house as soon as he sees his dad and Nico grins, spreading his arms out wide as he hurtles his little body into them.

"Hey, Zekey," I say, ruffling his hair and the little boy blinks hazel eyes that are a mirror image of his father's up at me.

"Hi, Mrs. Trixie," he says and he sticks his hand out for a high five.

"Is mommy home?" Zeke asks his dad and Nico nods, his eyes softening.

"I'll let you get home to her," I say as my husband comes down the walk with Zeke's bag in his hand.

"Did you have fun?" Nico asks him as he takes the bag from my husband.

"Yeah, Nicole and I played legos and Maxine made me an icee in her new toy!"

Zeke chatters on to Nico as he leads him over to his jeep and buckles the little boy inside. We all wave goodbye to them and I smile as I turn and wrap my arms around my husband.

"Any more of those icees left?"

"I'll make you one," he promises as he leads me inside where my girls instantly jump all over me.

The little puppy whines at the backdoor and Zeke hustles over to let her in. Zeke had said that he felt outnumbered so the girls and I decided to get him a puppy for Father's Day. I let them pick it out and they decided on a sheepadoodle who, it turns out, is a girl. I had laughed so hard when we found out and Zeke had just rolled his eyes. I know that he doesn't really care and that he loves our daughters and the puppy.

I'll admit, she is adorable but probably not the dog that Zeke would have picked out. He claims that he would and I know that he loves the dog. He named her Cherry Blossom, Cherry for short, and I'd be lying if my eyes didn't tear up when he told me he had picked a name.

I kneel down, scratching the puppy's ears as she jumps all over me, giving me kisses. The girls run off and soon Cherry is chasing after them, making them laugh and shriek. Zeke wraps his arm around my waist, leading me into the kitchen and over to the counter. He's already started on dinner and I smile at him.

"How did I get so lucky?"

"You walked into my tattoo shop," he says with a grin and I smile.

Thank god for that.

ABOUT THE AUTHOR

CONNECT WITH ME!

If you enjoyed this story, please consider leaving a review on Amazon or any other reader site or blog that you like. Don't forget to recommend it to your other reader friends.

If you want to chat with me, please consider joining my VIP list or connecting with me on one of my Social Media platforms. I love talking with each of my readers. Links below!

❥ VIP list
❥ shawhartbooks.com

ALSO BY SHAW HART

Remembering Valentine's Day

Finding Their Rhythm

Her Scottish Savior

Stealing Her

Hop Stuff

Dream Boat

Series by Shaw Hart

Telltale Heart Series

Bought and Paid For

His Miracle

Pretty Girl

Ash Mountain Pack Series

Growling For My Mate

Claiming My Mate

Mated For Life

Chasing My Mate

Protecting Our Mate

Love Note Series

Signing Off With Love

Care Package Love

Wrong Number, Right Love

Folklore Series

Kidnapped by Bigfoot

Loved by Yeti

Claimed by Her Sasquatch